Rhymes From The UK

Edited By Kelly Reeves

First published in Great Britain in 2020 by:

Young Writers
Remus House
Coltsfoot Drive
Peterborough
PE2 9BF
Telephone: 01733 890066
Website: www.youngwriters.co.uk

Printed and bound in the UK by BookPrintingUK
Website: www.bookprintinguk.com
YB0441N

FOREWORD

Here at Young Writers our defining aim is to promote the joys of reading and writing to children and young adults and we are committed to nurturing the creative talents of the next generation. By allowing them to see their own work in print we believe their confidence and love of creative writing will grow.

Out Of This World is our latest fantastic competition, specifically designed to encourage the writing skills of primary school children through the medium of poetry. From the high quality of entries received, it is clear that it really captured the imagination of all involved.

We are proud to present the resulting collection of poems that we are sure will amuse and inspire.

An absorbing insight into the imagination and thoughts of the young, we hope you will agree that this fantastic anthology is one to delight the whole family again and again.

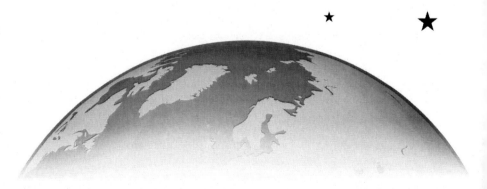

CONTENTS

St Cuthbert's RC Primary School, Withington

James McFarlane (11)	55
Damaris Gondwe (11)	56
Harini Sambaraju (10)	58
Ellie Buchanan (11)	60
Cece Blackwood (9)	61
Niamh Towey (10)	62
Amelia Greaves (8)	63
Raahil Mahmood (8)	64
Lexi Joyce (8)	65
Zuzanna Starostka (9)	66
Kyrillos Mebrahtom (7)	68
Martin Katamba (11)	69
Amelia Stimpson (8)	70
Paige Horrocks (6)	71
Mina Kaleem (8)	72
Aranza Lucia Luis De Gouveia (9)	73
Lilly Lawson (10)	74
Zaara Ali	75
Olivia Hinchliffe (11)	76
Adrian Navarro (8)	77
Natalia Aculey (7)	78
Presely Elsie Kasagga (6)	79
Elliott Oluwawomi (5)	80
Emily Doherty (6)	81

St Georges Church School, St Georges

Gabi Niec (10)	82
Izzy Hawley (10)	83
Spencer Craig (10)	84
Amie March (11)	85
Katie Pinner (10)	86

St Peter's CE Primary School, Harborne

Grace Littleford (9)	87
Mariele Lumbila (10)	88
Ellen Puzey (10)	90
Sana Hussain (10)	92

Christabel Reed (10)	94
Maya Sajjad (9)	96
Christie Johnson (11)	98
Suki Wu (7)	100
Emma Shakespeare (9)	101
Yeorgos Ford (7)	102
Mei Pihlaja (10)	103
Sara Luke (8)	104
Hanna Moradi (9)	105
Hateeka Hussain (10)	106
Zachary Mallen (9)	107
Matthew Pacheco (10)	108
Isobel Molesworth (11)	109
Abigail Mbobila (8)	110
Esinam Adom (10)	111
Hannah Manish (10)	112
Sofia Manea Vieira (7)	113
Aleah Brkic (7)	114
Gabrielle Challoner (7)	115
Mariam Zaakouk (8)	116
Deepika Kumari Sharma (7)	117

Widey Court Primary School, Crownhill

Lacie Humpage (8)	118
Owen Wren (8)	119
Oliver Tozer (8)	120
Georgia Horne (8)	121
Bethany Goodman (9)	122

THE POEMS

Park

A haiku

It is so much fun
There's lots of stuff to play with
They have trampolines.

Aimee Turner (7)

Beacon Primary Academy, Skegness

The Beach

A haiku

Majestic fun beach
In my Star Wars trunks jumping
It's hot on the beach.

Jack Flint (7)

Beacon Primary Academy, Skegness

Beach

A haiku

Riding the donkeys
Playing like I'm at the beach
The sand was so soft.

Byron Manning (7)

Beacon Primary Academy, Skegness

Beach

A haiku

The warm beach is fun
You can dig holes in the sand
Build amazing stuff.

Anna Paskejeva (7)
Beacon Primary Academy, Skegness

River

A haiku

They are big and long
They travel a long distance
They lead to the sea.

Oliver Epton (8)

Beacon Primary Academy, Skegness

Donkeys

A haiku

Donkeys on the beach
Good to ride and cuddle with
One is called Oscar.

Oscar Dickinson (8)
Beacon Primary Academy, Skegness

Beach

A haiku

The beach was sunny
Just like the stars in the sky
It was so calming.

Mia Jo-Ann Bee (8)
Beacon Primary Academy, Skegness

The Chip Shop

A haiku

The chip shop is good
There is a really big queue
Chips for everyone.

Jacob Roberts (8)

Beacon Primary Academy, Skegness

Arcades

A haiku

Entertaining rides
Winning prizes and tokens
Going out with friends.

Grace Marie Cunningham (8)

Beacon Primary Academy, Skegness

Fish And Chips

A haiku

Lovely salty chips
Cool sausages with them too
Red ketchup on top.

Evie Warren (7)
Beacon Primary Academy, Skegness

Arcade

A haiku

Big, noisy arcade
The arcade is fun and hot
You can win tickets.

Daisie Quickfall (7)
Beacon Primary Academy, Skegness

Arcades

A haiku

Fun for most parties
Smiling faces everywhere
Tired after fun.

Bobby Manning (7)

Beacon Primary Academy, Skegness

Fun Days Out

A haiku

Skegness is so fun
You can have a nice day out
KFC is great.

Joshua Ireland (7)
Beacon Primary Academy, Skegness

The Beach

A haiku

The warm, lovely beach
It is super-duper soft
It is amazing.

Nevaeh Drysdale (8)

Beacon Primary Academy, Skegness

Altitude 44

A haiku

Altitude is fun
Funny to watch people on
Nearly falling off.

Kiera Milnes (8)
Beacon Primary Academy, Skegness

The Planets

Shall I compare you to a cosmic world?
Home to me and home is the Earth
Up in the dance room is the dancer curled
Lying in a bed is a mother giving birth.

On Venus, the volcanoes give it a very big mass
Volcanoes spitting lava, spewing across the land
Fiery redness covered by a cloud of gas.
Though from the outside, it looks very bland.

Mars, the fourth planet from the sun, neighbour to
Earth
A deep red is its colour as it crosses
But its blank land doesn't have a lot of turf
And definitely doesn't have green plants and old
moss.

And many other planets past Mars will become
unreachable like stars
Burning a glowing red like the planet Mars.

Charlie Metcalf (9)
Newton Bluecoat CE Primary School, Newton With Scales

Super Stars And Marvellous Moon

The bright stars appear in the night sky blue,
You shine bright just like the stars in the sky,
The yellow stars are shining just like you,
The stars in the sky will catch your bright eye.

The cold, grey, cheesy moon turns day to night,
The moon gives a super, eye-catching glow,
When I look up, it might be a good sight,
I look up at the moon and see it flow.

I look up at the beautiful, bright star
The stars look like a diamond in the sky
I can see that the stars that glow are far
I know if I could reach you, I would try.

I can see the bright moon from where I live
I wish I knew what the bright stars would give.

Harriet Burrow (9)
Newton Bluecoat CE Primary School, Newton With Scales

Stars And Moon

The bright stars appear in the night sky blue,
You are my stars shining up above me,
The bright stars are shining up above you,
When I look up, I wonder what I see.

Shine up in the night sky, like you and me,
I love the stars, the moon that glows at night,
The moon and the stars are what you can see,
When I look up, it could be a good sight.

Glittering stars are up in the night sky,
The night-time comes, the stars and moon appear,
You are up there, up above, very very high,
When the stars appear, I will jump with fear.

The stars are up high, bright and far away,
The moon and stars twinkle in the night sky day.

Lucy Griffiths (9)
Newton Bluecoat CE Primary School, Newton With Scales

The Lava Burning Sun

Staring into the giant lava-burning sun
You could roast your own marshmallows on the rays
We could dance and play all day having fun
Lazy walks you make so there are perfect days.

A glowing glass sphere that turns like a ball
If something goes near you heat will appear
At night we wonder if it will ever fall
Your rays are so fast but you are not near.

The time we spend together brings happiness
If we orbit you, our lives will never end
Our lives so full of joy with very little stress
You are so hot you will help to descend.

You always fill my days with lots of heat
And I always wish someday we could meet.

Oliver Thackray (10)
Newton Bluecoat CE Primary School, Newton With Scales

The Moon And The Stars

Lighting up the sky with beautiful light,
The sky is filled with millions of silver stars,
Glowing so bright in the amazing night,
You won't believe this awesome moon is ours.

In the sky, the stars sit shining on us,
Looking up to the sky fills me with joy,
The light from our moon is so glorious,
So many words of praise I could employ.

You change shape so much, will you ever cease?
The stars in our sky are so wonderful
You're said to be cheese, so give me a piece,
Silver, shiny moon, your light is never dull.

You look like a big, shiny, silver pearl,
Every night you shine on every boy and girl.

Megan Byrne (10)
Newton Bluecoat CE Primary School, Newton With Scales

The Moon's Bright Light

I look up at the stunning moon at night,
Wondering if there could be life up there,
And then my curiosity takes flight,
The magnificent bright light makes me stare.

Down on the Earth shines a silvery glow,
Lighting up the sky so we don't get afraid,
The light follows me wherever I go,
And then I wonder when the moon was made.

Down on Earth, craters and holes can be seen,
Still the twinkling light shines down so bright,
What do those strange shapes on your surface
mean?
I am mesmerised by the stunning light.

We all see you up there in the night sky,
We all know that your light will never die.

Imogen Byrne (10)
Newton Bluecoat CE Primary School, Newton With Scales

The Sun

Take a dive into the realm of the sun
To meet the brightest star you will ever view
Setting like a golden penny to run
Back to the east, to make morning for you.

It's hot like fire and burns to the skin's touch
I wish I could have you around always
On happy days, we laugh and play so much
We have a perfect time together these days.

Pop up bright sun on this fine summer's day
All the people are waiting so please come
When it is sunny, we will think of May
For our happiness, we always need some.

The joy you bring gives me the reason to live
For everything in life is the food you give.

Olivia Hartley-Smith (10)
Newton Bluecoat CE Primary School, Newton With Scales

The Shining Sun

I find my happiness under the sun,
Lighting up the sky, making the light shine,
When you're under the sun, it's very fun,
The sun in the sky is very divine.

All day long the sun sits shining on us,
The sun in the sky shines upon us all,
Shining brightly in the sky is something it does,
Everybody says the sun is a ball.

Golden and glorious shining in the sky,
Dazzling, warming, it keeps us warm all day,
Every day the sun in the sky always comes by,
Some people say the sun is made of clay.

The sun shines brightly, it almost blinds me,
The sun is bright and that is what you see.

Abbie Ely (10)
Newton Bluecoat CE Primary School, Newton With Scales

Starry Sky

Looking out at the starry, bright night sky
You shine on us through the air, cold and clear
Long-lasting, I wish you would never die
Like shooting stars do in our atmosphere.

Our daytime star comes up in the far east
And travels across to set in the west
We would miss it if it should ever cease
For our lighting and warmth is the best.

The beautiful patterns of the night stars
Making us think of stories and heroes
The gods and goddesses, Venus and Mars
Orion, the hunter, with arrows and bows.

Oh beautiful sun, we love your bright light
But so do the twinkling stars of night.

Josef Cosgrove-Highton (10)
Newton Bluecoat CE Primary School, Newton With Scales

The Sun

As the sun sinks like a golden penny,
Lighting up the sky with a friendly smile,
It is like a giant, fluffy teddy
For you, I would travel the extra mile.

The sun and rain makes a pretty rainbow
The sun gives us wonderful holidays,
The sun is not like a big ball of snow,
But far too bright, on it we cannot gaze.

The sun is a giant gas ball of fire
When the sun shines bright it gives us the light,
The sun is like a big, round, orange tyre,
When the sun goes down it becomes the night.

I wonder where the sun will go this night
The amazing sun will give us the light.

Lacey Horvath (9)
Newton Bluecoat CE Primary School, Newton With Scales

Shall I Compare You To The Orange Sun?

Shall I compare you to the orange sun?
The big sun is hot like burning lava
If you walk on the sun, it's very fun
The big giant sun is like our father.

The sun is a warrior, it can survive
The sun is like a burning, shining star
Without the sun, nothing will be alive
The sun is very big and very far.

The sun gives light to all of the planets
The sun gives life to the whole universe
The sun might have some kind of rock called granite
The sun could possibly be a good curse.

The sun is very hot, it's red and cool
The sun is like a hot, burning pool.

Nathan Eastwood (9)
Newton Bluecoat CE Primary School, Newton With Scales

The Moon

Friendly, big lump of hard and dusty rock
Smiling down on the Earth at us below
Did you experience a great big shock
When men onto your surface did go?

I love looking up in the bright night sky
To see what shows you are making
Will you be full round like a pizza pie
Or a tiny, silver light?

We know that your rays of silver
Are not made by you but come from our star, the
sun
But we are glad that you have a time slot
That makes us able to have a night run.

Moon, lovely moon,
Our best friend in all space
Thank you for keeping the Earth in its place.

Annie Fare (9)
Newton Bluecoat CE Primary School, Newton With Scales

Sun, Beautiful Sun

Shall I compare you to lava burning?
For I see you and I could be scorched
When I go near you, I will be yearning
In the heat of the day, I am a torch.

As you shine, the plants sprout beautifully
Strong in a wonderful, pure, true red glow
As you go down, you go down gracefully
Like a dancer who sways in water's flow.

When you come up with a bright orange light
You make my day a happy day again
The orange light is very, very bright
And I think I am high up on a plane.

You always make my day with lots of heat
And I always wish we could someday meet.

Kian Sim (10)
Newton Bluecoat CE Primary School, Newton With Scales

The Planets Around The Sun

Mercury, closest to the hot sun
The messenger into the wilderness
Venus, god of love, is the only one
God Mars, when it comes to war, is the best.

Jupiter, the biggest ball of gas there is
Saturn owns precious debris rings
Uranus sparkles with a super fizz
About Neptune, we don't know many things.

The dwarf planet's small, the gas giants are big
They all orbit the sun and so do we
In orbit, the planets do a nice jig
The thought of them gives me all my glee.

All the good planets above us
Imagine what's out there and don't make a fuss.

Callum Dougherty (9)
Newton Bluecoat CE Primary School, Newton With Scales

Our Solar System

The sun gives us all its wonderful light
And is our galaxy's biggest star
The moon is seen in the night and is bright
And from here is said to be very far.

Mercury is extremely cold at night
Venus is known for being very warm
Earth, like Goldilocks, for us is just right
Mars would be a doomed place for a warm home.

Jupiter, the biggest planet of all
Saturn owns a bright and beautiful ring
Uranus is the opposite of small
Neptune is a great gust of blue wind.

Don't include the former planet, Pluto
I have told you now so now you will know.

Lucas Wearden (10)
Newton Bluecoat CE Primary School, Newton With Scales

The Planets

Mercury is a tiny shaped ball
Its days are short and its width is quite long
Venus is big and is not small at all
Its heat and gas sounds like a loud birdsong
Mars has a warm day and very cold night
It has a very live volcano there
Jupiter has many moons and great sights
It being big isn't nice and it's not fair
Saturn has a ring of very hard rock
It has a surface that is super long
Uranus is cold and longer than a sock
If you call it rude names, it knows you're wrong
There are many planets out there in space
Just because some are small is not the case.

Jamie Irvine (10)
Newton Bluecoat CE Primary School, Newton With Scales

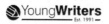
Comparison

Shall I compare you to the shining sun?
You are nearly as bright and as hot
When night falls and the realms of sol are done
You shine brightly above us, a diamond dot.

You are described as the moon of love
A god was named after your glowing light
You shine and glow and are way up above
Giving me a marvellous great sight.

For you are from another dimension
A galaxy that is very far away
Never in doubt, you shine with a mission
To warm our soul on a very special day.

The best day of my amazing, crazy life
Is spent having fun with you in my life.

Seth Whitehead (10)
Newton Bluecoat CE Primary School, Newton With Scales

Wondrous Sun

The sun is as red as a fireball
The sun is making the morning for you
The sun is rising above the night sky
The sun is golden and is always true
When I look up, I see the boiling sun
The sun is lighting up the massive world
That gives me wondrous warmth and fun
Creating a feeling that can make me swirl
When you leave me every dark, lonely night
I cannot wait 'til the daytime arrives
So that I can see you and feel your light
For in your presence, we all truly thrive
You create life for us all to enjoy
Giving us love and strength, you make a boy.

Jack Acourt (9)
Newton Bluecoat CE Primary School, Newton With Scales

The Sun

Vanishing into the ocean floor now
I got burnt on the beach while sunbathing
I wonder, I wonder, I wonder how
The sun, the sun, the sun is amazing.

The sun is a teeny tiny star
The sun is life, the sun is dust
You shine on us from the sky afar
I hope that we don't explode.

The sun brings life, the sun brings me today
It makes me happy, full of joy
Giving me the chance to have fun and play
And become a strong and healthy young boy.

When night comes we say goodbye to the sun
Making sure that our day is now done.

Harley Traynor (10)
Newton Bluecoat CE Primary School, Newton With Scales

In Space

The sun is red, just like Mars
It is not a chocolate bar
The sun is a fireball, it is far
It will explode when it is ready.

Earth is blue, Earth is green
Moon brightens the night
It looks like cheese
It is a satellite.

The planets create a solar system
We gaze up to the heavens to see them
That shine upon us and have a mission
Like a ruby, you glow like a gem.

What we do without undying love
Bringing joy to all you shine bright above.

Charlie Baugh (9)
Newton Bluecoat CE Primary School, Newton With Scales

Australian Bush Fires

A ustralia is under attack
U se fire extinguishers
S tay away
T wists and turns
R ound and round
A pple trees burnt
L ies from the government
I magine a brighter day
A rghhhh, a fire!
N egative response.

B ecause of this, they are scared
U se fire blankets
S hout for help
H ide and run when it is safe.

F ires are growing
I n Australia
R un, hide, quick
E eeek, a fire!
S ea levels are rising, more danger.

Hannah Lodge (8)
Rettendon Primary School, Rettendon Common

Minecraft

M oo cows are in their moo cage

I n Minecraft, you can do anything

N o, my cows have escaped, I cannot milk them

E very time I make a mistake in Minecraft

C raft everything in the world

R ebuild everything if a Creeper explodes

A horse will take you where you want to go

F ish are fascinating to look at

T omorrow I will build more.

Charlie Lawrence (8)
Rettendon Primary School, Rettendon Common

My BFF

M iracle! I know you are!
Y ou're amazing, like the world!

B elieve in yourself
F riends forever and ever
F abulous friends forever.

A mazing Alice
L ucky I found her
I will always be your best friend
C an get through everything together
E ven better than the world.

Chelsea Barford (10)
Rettendon Primary School, Rettendon Common

Biggest Land Animals

E ating leaves, that's their diet,

L arge animal, the biggest land one,

E xciting to watch,

P eople are scared but they don't hurt you,

H ats? Do they wear hats?

A huge animal,

N o way! They kill people!

T ime flies when you watch them,

S mall babies but huge adults.

Elena Ward (9)

Rettendon Primary School, Rettendon Common

The Woods

T ents set out quickly now,
H ow are you doing friends?
E mily quickly, night is falling.

W ow, this is nice, get your torches
O w! That hurt, what happened Jim?
O w! Oh no, a strange man!
D uo up and go back
S ounds better now, goodnight!

Caitlyn Weedon (8)
Rettendon Primary School, Rettendon Common

Rubbish

R usty road full of junk,

U seful plastic bottles,

B ins full up with clutter,

B roken glass as smashed as a broken window,

I n streets, it's very smelly,

S tinky smelly bins everywhere,

H orrible smells in the air.

Amelie Othman (9)
Rettendon Primary School, Rettendon Common

Rubbish

R idiculous, revolting rubbish

U nless people tidy up

B ins that are smelly as rotten eggs

B ad wrapper scattered on the floor

I t is so icky so tidy up

S melly things in places

H orrible things clean up.

Isabel Burke (9)

Rettendon Primary School, Rettendon Common

Litter!

L ots of mess on the floor
I n the streets and not in the bin
T he revolting rubbish is really messy
T here is too much litter all around us
E veryone should throw it in the bin
R ubbish will then be gone.

Izzy Gardner (10)
Rettendon Primary School, Rettendon Common

Rubbish

R evolting debris
U glier than the rest
B in it all
B urger buns on the floor
I nky pens leaking on your feet
S ooty soda pops, nowhere near the bin
H ave you cleaned it up yet?

Hugo Ride (10)

Rettendon Primary School, Rettendon Common

Trash!

T he Litter Muncher always tidies the village
R ubbish is discarded
A fter a few days, he was very tired
S nacks all over the village get munched up
H e never gives up as a World Cup footballer.

Karim Shah Ramjean
Rettendon Primary School, Rettendon Common

Litter

L ook at this rubbish,
I t smells disgusting,
T o the dump,
T o never see again,
E rm, it's disgusting
R oads full of rubbish, smelling like ten bin bags.

Matthew Hiscott (8)

Rettendon Primary School, Rettendon Common

Trash

T he people put their litter in the bin

R evolting banana skins

A really smelly day

S crap paper everywhere

H orrible banana skins look like a rotten apple.

Jason Lowrie (9)

Rettendon Primary School, Rettendon Common

Litter

L eftover food
I s the worst thing ever
T ip as bright as the sun
T aps leaking everywhere
E www! Banana skins, yuck!
R ubble all over the place.

Finley Ranson (9)

Rettendon Primary School, Rettendon Common

Trash

T he bin is where you put your waste

R evolting garbage everywhere

A really horrible day today

S o gross! It smells like a pig

H elp, too much rubbish!

Freddie Seymour (9)

Rettendon Primary School, Rettendon Common

Dragons

D angerous creatures
R oaring at the sky
A long, scaly tail
G reen and scary eyes
O n its back long spikes grow
N ear a land no one knows.

Freya Salih-Phipps (9)
Rettendon Primary School, Rettendon Common

Trash

T he dirty village is not pretty,

R ubbish is smelly as a bin,

A ll of the town is dirty,

S mall piles of litter,

H ard cardboard, as hard as wood.

Mia Key (8)
Rettendon Primary School, Rettendon Common

Litter!

L ittle as dust,

I n the sea,

T he thing floats like a dead bee,

T he fish are dying,

E verywhere,

R un little fishes, run, run, run!

Elsie Gorecki (9)

Rettendon Primary School, Rettendon Common

Trash!

T he rubbish is everywhere

R un through it

A s fast as you can

S he climbed to the top of the pile

H e was very scared like a lost child.

Hudson Daly (9)
Rettendon Primary School, Rettendon Common

Bins

B ins, we all put litter in them
I t's not good to drop litter
N o littering because it would be
S melly as a sewer.

Tyler McCreadie (8)
Rettendon Primary School, Rettendon Common

Japan, Japan

Japan, Japan with its cherry blossom trees,
Japan, Japan, it's my cup of tea,
Japan, Japan, what a place to be!
Japan, Japan, there's a lot to see
Japan, Japan, has lots of lights,
Japan, Japan, so many sights.

Delicious ramen noodles, what a treat!
Everywhere you go there's food to eat
Fried rice, sushi and chicken meat
These are foods you find on every street
Arcades, manga, anime too
Japanese lakes are sky blue!

Japan, Japan with its cherry blossom trees,
Japan, Japan, it's my cup of tea,
Japan, Japan, what a place to be!
Japan, Japan, there's a lot to see
Japan, Japan, has lots of lights,
Japan, Japan, so many sights.

James McFarlane (11)
St Cuthbert's RC Primary School, Withington

Terrific Trees

Trees are less by the day because of greed,
Some chopped down daily because of monetary need,
It's time we took care of our terrific trees,
Because they give us air that we all need,
But some still don't care,
And it is very unfair,
Some still don't care about pollution,
That's why we urgently need a solution,
If we continue chopping down trees,
Soon there will be no clean air to breathe,
We need to preserve trees for our future generation,
As they deserve an environmentally clean nation,
We can save the planet if we all pitch in,
To curb the high levels of air pollution so far seen,
We only have one life and one planet,
And this is the only time to act that we will ever get,
So let's take action now! And we all know how,
Plant more trees and say no to cutting down trees,
They have a purpose in our lives,

They without doubt make us stay alive,
Please! Please! Please!
Don't let the terrific trees die!

Damaris Gondwe (11)
St Cuthbert's RC Primary School, Withington

The Four Seasons

Spring, summer, autumn and winter
This is the order of the year.

Spring!
We celebrate Easter,
We don't turn on the heaters,
Flowers and trees start to grow,
We wished this happened a long time ago.

Summer!
Go to the beach and build a sandcastle,
But making it strong is an absolute hassle,
Then play in the hot sun
And have lots of fun.

Autumn!
Leaves fall down,
This happens in every single town,
It rains all the time,
And we don't get much sunshine.

Winter!
Snow falls like glitter,

We have a nice Christmas dinner,
We just want to rest,
And feel like we're in a bird's nest.

Spring, summer, autumn and winter
Four seasons of the year
Can go by and come.

Harini Sambaraju (10)
St Cuthbert's RC Primary School, Withington

Let's Make A Change

Let's make a change,
We love our Earth,
We love our mums who gave birth,
Let's make a change,
Our forests are turning into ash,
Let's just donate a little cash,
Let's make a change,
Supermarkets, why so much plastic?
Just use some elastic,
Let's make a change,
Watching our Earth dying slow,
It's just hard for me to let go,
Let's make a change,
Electric cars blew me away,
Think about how they save the world every day,
Let's make a change,
Do you really want to see the world go bye-bye?
Come on, let's at least try.

My name's Ellie Buchanan
And I will make a big change.

Ellie Buchanan (11)
St Cuthbert's RC Primary School, Withington

Save The Planet

If you see plastic on the ground,
Pick it up without a frown,
We are setting fire to our forests and homes,
Cutting trees isn't a joke,
Chemicals floating in the air,
Plastic in the ocean kills me and no one cares,
It hurts to see what our future holds,
Because if we carry on, there is no hope,
Every day animals die, people leave homes,
Because of forest fires,
Koalas burn and firemen save animals,
Set fire and need to escape,
Woodcutters make paper and make the situation worse,
Whilst sea turtles choke and rhinos get hurt,
All of this is happening to our Earth,
Take action now because it's just going to get worse.

Cece Blackwood (9)
St Cuthbert's RC Primary School, Withington

Spectre's Visit

The spectre is a disturbing fiend,
It stirs trouble at night,
It edges in on darkness' wing,
Glimpsed in the dawning light.

The spectre's breath is in my hair,
I keep my eyes shut tight,
The spectre's breath is everywhere,
Unseen in pale moonlight.

The spectre preys on children's dreams,
It embodies them with dread,
It guffaws at its evil schemes,
And crams them in my head.

The spectre's like a sinister demon,
It lingers, it howls, it spits
It's midnight I detest the most,
The hour my spectre visits.

Niamh Towey (10)
St Cuthbert's RC Primary School, Withington

What To Do With Litter

If you see a tin, put it in the bin
If there's not a bin around, pick it up from off the
ground,
Some people do it with a frown face
As they are thinking about all the poor animals
choking
Some people think I'm joking
About litter when I'm not
I wish I could get a pot
And make a potion out of it
It's still not good if you bury rubbish in a pit
As worms and some bugs live underground
We should do a vote and write a note
To all the people who don't care about animals
Save the planet!

Amelia Greaves (8)
St Cuthbert's RC Primary School, Withington

Rainforest

R ain falls down from the sky, making the plants grow

A nimals awake from their slumber in the morning dew

I n the understory, mammals, reptiles and amphibians live

N ests full of little birds chirping for their lunch

F orest floors covered with roots

O rangutans help their babies to climb

R ed, green, yellow parrots and many other birds

E ggs emerging from their shells

S nakes slithering around the trees

T hese trees are where the forest creatures reside.

Raahil Mahmood (8)
St Cuthbert's RC Primary School, Withington

The Rainforest

The rainforest is bright, brighter than a light
Every colour of the rainbow, you can even see at
night
All different animals playing happily in my sight
Wow, I saw a Macaw flying higher than a kite.

Swinging through the trees was a chimpanzee
"Hello Miss Joyce!" Aww, he was very polite.

Oh, and the flowers smelt so sweet,
I probably could pick some to take home to eat.

Now it's time to get ready for school
So a big hug from a sloth and I will be back soon.

Lexi Joyce (8)
St Cuthbert's RC Primary School, Withington

Save Our Planet

Save our planet
Everyone says!

Save our planet
Let's do our best!

Don't use the plastic
Don't waste too much.

Save our planet
Let's win this match!

I am gonna tell you
In a few words...

Save our planet
Save our birds
Save our plants
And beautiful green lands!

Do it together
Let's do it now,
This must be the best plan!

Do this for our future
We need your help
To live happily
On our Earth!

Zuzanna Starostka (9)

St Cuthbert's RC Primary School, Withington

Family

Family, I love
In the valley of love
Love of family is so strong
It's not for some time,
It's for throughout and so long,
I oh so love my family so much,
I will forever stay with them,
'Cause they are my true support
Family teaching us many good things
And family help us to do sharing and caring about
our people
Thank God for giving me a family
Everyone needs to love their family
My family prepares us food when we are hungry
And when we are not hungry.

Kyrillos Mebrahtom (7)
St Cuthbert's RC Primary School, Withington

Autumn Poem

I can see the leaves in yellow, red and brown,
A shower of them sprinkles down,
Some of them give up and fall,
While others stay high above all.

I feel the breeze, fragrant and cool,
And once again, I'm stuck in school,
Although the breeze is refreshing and slick,
Never underestimate it, it can make you sick.

I can't smell the stench of beautiful flowers,
Especially in the rainy showers,
I can smell the drenched green grass.

Martin Katamba (11)
St Cuthbert's RC Primary School, Withington

The Galaxy World

Looking through my telescope, space doesn't seem so far?
Watching light come zooming past from Jupiter and Mars
Once you look past the full moon and all the closest stars
Then onto a new galaxy to explore near and far comets shooting
Past the sky, leaving a shimmering trail behind
Then I hear my name being called and back down to Earth
Zoom! Dreaming of the next chance to explore the night-time sky.

Amelia Stimpson (8)
St Cuthbert's RC Primary School, Withington

My Two Sisters

My two sisters are very bad,
Sometimes they make me very sad
They shout and scream
Throw tantrums too
They make me scream until I am blue
But I love them
With all my heart
No matter how much
They try to start
Sometimes they are naughty
And sometimes they are good
But every day, they jump in the mud
One has brown eyes
And one has blue
But I always say
I love you.

Paige Horrocks (6)
St Cuthbert's RC Primary School, Withington

Polluted World

Dirt, dirt everywhere
Not a clean spot anywhere
Whenever I go out to meet Max,
The road is full of plastic bags
Right above in the sky,
Not a star can be seen by the eye
In the beautiful oceans lie,
Thousands of animals that every day die
Cut all the trees, they say,
The world will turn black and grey!
All I want to say my friend,
Is the world will come to an end!

Mina Kaleem (8)
St Cuthbert's RC Primary School, Withington

Animals In Your Heart

Animals sleep all sound,
Huddled together in their house
Every child likes pets,
To have some fun and play with them,
Dogs and cats bark and meow,
As they catch squirrels in the dark
They like to play and run around
As every child in a playground
As this story ends, don't be sad,
As you might get a pet in your house!

Aranza Lucia Luis De Gouveia (9)
St Cuthbert's RC Primary School, Withington

Peacarni Bird

Peacarni bird is the best of all,
Don't talk to this bird or you will make it call,
It lives on a planet called Timberooh,
Do you want to see it? I hope you do,
Look inside this nest,
Don't be frightened, it will be a test,
Now you have looked, run, run, run!
I bet you will end up in its tum, tum, tum!

Lilly Lawson (10)
St Cuthbert's RC Primary School, Withington

My School

We have some rules
We have some rules
Rules to keep us safe in school
Inside voices, walking feet
Don't touch or bother
The friends we meet
If you listen to your teacher
You can make your good future
Apples and oranges are so tasty
My St Cuthbert's School is the best.

Zaara Ali
St Cuthbert's RC Primary School, Withington

When I Am Older

When I am older, I want to go to space,
To see the world that is right above our face,
When I am older, I want to be a nurse,
To stop the worst,
When I am older, I will audition
To be a magician,
When I am older,
I hope the world is the best place to be.

Olivia Hinchliffe (11)
St Cuthbert's RC Primary School, Withington

UNICEF Children

U nbelievable work by UNICEF

N ot so lucky like us

I ncredibly bad diseases

C an be a bit hard sometimes if you're one of them

E qual rights for all the kids

F orward working together to make the world a better place.

Adrian Navarro (8)
St Cuthbert's RC Primary School, Withington

Mystical And Magical

Love is invisible
Fire is ice
Dreams are now possible
Evil people could be nice
When did you know?
It could be true
But the secrets are for you
Not for me, not for he
But mankind can see.

Natalia Aculey (7)
St Cuthbert's RC Primary School, Withington

About My Friends

I like my friends
Because they play with me a lot
I like them very much
They're so kind
I play outside with my friends
We have so much fun
My friend, Tara, is as beautiful as a rainbow.

Presely Elsie Kasagga (6)
St Cuthbert's RC Primary School, Withington

The Star

Up, up in the sky
Way, way high
My eyes shine
Just like a star
My eyes twinkle
And winkle
Just like a star
In the midnight sky
Way, way high.

Elliott Oluwawomi (5)
St Cuthbert's RC Primary School, Withington

The Hungry Aliens

The aliens in the sky
Make a huge, gooey pie
They gobble it all up
Like a hungry little pup.

Emily Doherty (6)
St Cuthbert's RC Primary School, Withington

Dreams

There was once a young girl,
Whose voice was like a pearl,
She dreamt to sing,
When she went bing!
The girl hoped her dream would come true,
If not, her heart went blue,
She could see the shooting star shine,
In the deep, dark sky,
Sarah thought of a wish,
That was not a fish,
Her fans would clap,
And she would tap,
The little girl sang,
With her gang,
It was like a tune of magic,
And it wouldn't be tragic.

Gabi Niec (10)
St Georges Church School, St Georges

The Great Friendship Poem

What a joy it is to have a friend just like you,
I hope you know that our friendship is true,
No matter what happens, I will always be by your side,
We will always be by each other's sides.

Our friendship is a priceless gift,
No one can replace it,
This friendship can't be bought or sold.

Thanks for being there when I needed you the most,
Your friendship means the most,
This is what I want you to know.

Izzy Hawley (10)
St Georges Church School, St Georges

Football Fever

F antastic football
O ffside rules
O ver the goal it goes
T eam spirit
B race yourself
A ction-packed
L ovely game
L ater losers.

F ull-time whistle blown
E xciting atmosphere
V ocal supporters
E verlasting chants
R epresenting your football club.

Spencer Craig (10)
St Georges Church School, St Georges

Two Lost Princesses

Two lost princesses in a stormy weather
One called Ellie and one called Heather.

Battling through the storm
Wishing they were never born,

"Why did we start this?" they said
With pain coming right to their heads.

Making the whole village suffer
With nothing to do but try to stay buffer.

Amie March (11)
St Georges Church School, St Georges

Weather Is Good, Weather Is Bad

Weather is good, weather is bad,
Sometimes weather can drive you mad.

As it rains on you, it rains on me,
It rains on earth, land and sea.

The sun is warm, the sun is hot,
We miss it when we have it not.

Weather is good, weather is bad,
Sometimes weather can drive you mad.

Katie Pinner (10)
St Georges Church School, St Georges

The Lonely Star

A star shone in the night sky, lonely as can be,
And it counted the stars in the distance... one, two,
three,
This little star was sad,
For it had no mom or dad,
No brother, no sister,
No Mrs, no Mr,
Alone in the darkness, the star started to cry,
But nobody heard him, so nobody asked why,
Then a shooting star heard him far, far away,
And it zoomed off to find him, come what may,
Then she saw him, all alone,
Crying his eyes out in a high-pitched tone,
She raced towards him, as fast as she could,
He asked if she'd help him and she said she would
They played lots of games, in fact they played four,
And the lonely star was not lonely anymore,
Then they went on an adventure, for she knew the
way,
And they still are best friends right to this day.

Grace Littleford (9)
St Peter's CE Primary School, Harborne

Change Our Ways, Change Our World

We're killing the Earth, we tell everyone
But no one believes us because we are young
Our forests are turning to ash in this second
Ask all Americans, they'll tell you about it
They'll tell you how they have lost all their homes
How Trump turns a blind eye and tweets on his phone
Global warming is an expensive, little choke
For the last time, it's not a joke
Our factories are working and toxins emitting
The ozone is crumbling and we won't stop
Putting chemicals in what we're trying to breathe
Our future is stolen and we are the thieves
The icebergs are melting, the coral reefs are dying
The sea levels are rising and no one's advising
Can't you see that our water source pollutes?
But did you know we are the brutes?
Don't come to me when your child can't think
Or when a tiger becomes extinct
Don't come to me when your jacket ain't clean

The endangered list is now 41,416
Dear 2045, I don't think we're gonna survive
And if you end up hearing this poem,
I just wanna say sorry.

Mariele Lumbila (10)
St Peter's CE Primary School, Harborne

The Day War Came

The day war came was like any other:
Rivers of plastic baking in the heat,
The weary man on the radio reporting more bushfires,
The remaining grumbling animals pleading for change.
Change was coming but not for the good.

War came in trucks as black as midnight,
Confusing me with guns and shouts in a foreign language.
It came and took the food and water from us,
Anyone who fought back vanished in a flash.

War came and closed the school,
Boys learnt to fight and girls to cook and clean,
War caused more floods and stole all the water,
Burnt more fires and produced more fear.

One night, war got worse, much worse,
Flames licked up the city skyline,
As they built their empire.

We went into hiding,
They said we would be safe but they said war
wouldn't happen.

Rat-a-tat-tat
The door moaned in agony as they knocked it
down with one blow
Footsteps approaching my hiding place
War reaches out towards me...

Ellen Puzey (10)
St Peter's CE Primary School, Harborne

Let's Fight Against Bullying!

Bullying has to come to an end
Let's all be nice and let's all be friends
Bullying is bad, bullying is not cool
Bullying is sad, bullying does not belong in our
school
It doesn't make you strong
It doesn't make you tough, bullying is wrong
And we've all had enough
Bullying has to stop,
Bullying doesn't make you on top
Regardless of culture, regardless of race,
Regardless of colour, regardless of faith, everyone
is equal in my face
We're all a team, let's be happy
There's no need to be mean, we're one big family
You should know bullying hurts
It starts with one word and then it gets worse
If you are being bullied, make sure you ask for help
We all have each other, you are not by yourself

Don't give up, you are a fighter
'Blowing out someone else's candle doesn't make yours shine any brighter'.

Sana Hussain (10)
St Peter's CE Primary School, Harborne

Cookie Cat, The Rocket Cat

Cookie Cat, she's a rocket cat
Cookie Cat, she's a rocket cat
Cookie Cat was sent to space when she was one year old
Arriving in a spaceship that was big and bold
She zoomed across comets and some shooting stars,
It was like her spaceship was a racing car!
A few years passed and for some unknown reason,
Cookie Cat's ship crashed, in the new season!
But Cookie Cat was brave and decided what to do,
"I'll go back down as a rocket cat!"
Cookie Cat, she's a rocket cat
Cookie Cat, she's a rocket cat
You may be wondering, how does she do that?
She collected some stardust and sprinkled it all over
She headed down to Earth, getting closer and closer
Is it a plane? Is it a bird?

No, it's Cookie Cat, the rocket cat!
Cookie Cat, she's a rocket cat
Cookie Cat, the rocket cat!

Christabel Reed (10)
St Peter's CE Primary School, Harborne

Rainforest

Underneath the canopy,
The rustle of busy leaves,
Listening to the symphony,
The symphony of life.

Chittering and chattering of cheeky monkeys,
Squawking of splendid birds of paradise,
A lazy sloth snoozing and snoring among trees,
Hummingbirds humming wonderful tunes.

Jewels hanging on thin branches glinting in the
sun,
Plump and juicy, smelling ever so refreshing,
Waiting to be plucked, one by one,
Waiting to be munched, to be squashed to a pulp.

The swishing and swaying of the lively trees,
Splishing and splashing of babbling streams,
The rustle and the bustle of dried up leaves,
And the gentle howling of the rainforest breeze.

Underneath the canopy,
The rustle of busy leaves,

Listen to the symphony,
The symphony of life.

Maya Sajjad (9)
St Peter's CE Primary School, Harborne

The Fight

The eerie silence was angry as the soldiers
marched up to their glee fields,
Their armour was a scarlet blood-red, especially
their shields,
And their clothes were shades of grey and black.

They shared a plastic smile between themselves,
And gestured each other to the fields they hated
the most,
They were missing the post,
And the warm, crisp fires back at home.

The fight had now begun,
And towards the battle the soldiers did run,
Fierce, large boulders and shots launched across
the air,
And the atmosphere was tense.

But they hadn't won, not yet,
Numerous guns were still in sight,
And despite their fear, they didn't take flight,

The last shot was fired,
And what happened next was a miracle.

They had won.

Christie Johnson (11)
St Peter's CE Primary School, Harborne

Zombie Time

Get in line, it's the zombie rhyme
Get those bags, but they have some rags
Zombies aren't strong or like King Kong
Zombies are hard to find and they definitely can't
read your mind
Different zombies are dangerous or sweet and
they might want some raw meat
Some are high, some are low, whichever one it is,
shoot them with a bow
Some have teams while others eat beans
If your zombie eats beans, be prepared they might
fart in their jeans
Some watch TV and others can't see
If it can't see, fight it, but if it watches TV, it might
be blind just a little bit
Some are disgusting and some are adjusting
They look like a crook and smell like a book
So bye-bye for now and I will take a bow
The zombies might cry but soon, they're going to
die.

Suki Wu (7)
St Peter's CE Primary School, Harborne

The Haunted House

I stepped into a big, old house one day,
When a group of bats swept against my head,
Skeletons sitting in the corner of the room,
Spiders crawling around,
An icy gust of wind blew the door closed,
I was all alone,
"Help! Help!" I cried, but all was silent and still,
A huge longcase clock opposite me,
Then suddenly, the squeak of a big, grey, grizzly
mouse flashed past me,
I then turned towards it and its yellowy-brown
teeth snarled at me,
I took a deep breath,
Immediately, the clock struck twelve,
The skeletons disappeared, the mouse had gone,
Everything was normal!

Emma Shakespeare (9)
St Peter's CE Primary School, Harborne

Space

All black in space, there is endless space,
A labyrinth of stars and still plenty of space,
Trails of planets, some are big, some are small,
Our one, the Earth, is bigger than the store,
Gazillions of miles of pure black space,
Space here and space there and who knows what
lives there,
It could be yetis or a bear,
Maybe holes to other dimensions or just space
extensions,
There could be aliens, big and small, tall and short,
Some might even snort, gross!
They could be made out of slime, goo or skin,
But nobody has seen one or two, three or four,
But they could eat you so watch out at home.

Yeorgos Ford (7)
St Peter's CE Primary School, Harborne

True Or False?

Climate change, true or false?
Some people think it's bad,
Some people think it's a sign,
Some people act,
Some people think it's a joke,
But is it really?

Climate change, true or false?
Some people help,
Some people change their whole lives,
Some people protest and miss out on school,
Some people kill animals to extinction,
Some people help deforestation,
Some people say it's for the 'better of us',
But is it really?

Mei Pihlaja (10)
St Peter's CE Primary School, Harborne

I Love...

I love my teddy bear
I cuddle him when I'm cold
I'll never stop loving him
Even when I'm old.

I love rainbows, they are
Colourful and bright
They make the sky look pretty
And are an amazing sight.

I love dogs, they are so cute
And love to play
I hope my daddy gets me one
It would be a fantastic day.

I love flowers, they are
So pretty and bright
After a long winter,
They are a beautiful sight.

Sara Luke (8)
St Peter's CE Primary School, Harborne

My Family!

To family, I love you a lot
But you are very weird
So I had to tell you this:

You all are very kind
You always help any time
You get crazy when I get things wrong
I just want to remind you I am very strong
But you got to know, it's all right to get things
wrong.

Mum, you help me,
Dad is funny,
Sister plays with me.

I hope you learned about my family,
But this is a secret between you and me!

Hanna Moradi (9)

St Peter's CE Primary School, Harborne

Family

It's sometimes hard to put into words,
Just what I'd like to say
But God gave us a special family that I can call my own
We are all from the same tree, but different branches
It's like a patchwork quilt, with kindness gently sewn
Each piece an original with beauty of its own
The care of our family is so strong
It is not for some time,
It is for throughout and long,
I am who I am because of all those who shaped me.

Hateeka Hussain (10)
St Peter's CE Primary School, Harborne

The Monster In The Basement!

One day, a boy called Henry went down to the basement to unpack (he'd just moved house.) He heard a thump! "What was that?" asked Henry. He saw a red eye pop out and then 20 pointy teeth as sharp as glass. As quick as a flash, the monster gobbled him up!

Henry's mum came down and said, "Henry love, is everything okay?"

"Yes," replied the monster as if nothing had happened. Henry's mum walked back upstairs!

Zachary Mallen (9)

St Peter's CE Primary School, Harborne

Mother Nature

N ature is a mystery that only works side by side with

A nimals, trees and Mother Nature herself

T rust is built between them to create an

U nique comprehension and working within them, they can

R ebuild what the humans have been destroying

E xploring new horizons and destroying forests is what the humans have been doing more often lately, unfortunately.

Matthew Pacheco (10)

St Peter's CE Primary School, Harborne

Silver Swan

One cold winter
A small swan flew
Up over the clouds
And into the blue.

One cold winter night
A small silver swan
Flew over the lake
With any fear? None.

One cold winter night
The swan flew away
Because the night
Was beginning to fray.

One cold winter night
A small swan flew
Up over the clouds
And into the blue.

Isobel Molesworth (11)
St Peter's CE Primary School, Harborne

My Alien Poem

Aliens are strange
You will never know what they like
Some might even know how to ride a bike
Some are blue, some are green
Some might even know the Queen
Aliens often go mad
Most aliens are really bad
I think that aliens could maybe fly
Most of them are really sly
Some are dry, some are wet
No one has discovered aliens yet.

Abigail Mbobila (8)
St Peter's CE Primary School, Harborne

A Friend You Need

Come and play with me
I am kind but daring
You will love me, just wait and see
I am very thoughtful you know
You can trust me
Don't be afraid
I'm not like any other
I'm here through good and bad times
You will always have me by your side
So come and find your true self
That lies within.

Esinam Adom (10)
St Peter's CE Primary School, Harborne

Dreamful Dreams

Dreams are great adventures
And have different types of textures
Dreams can be funny
And tickle the tummy
They can also be tense
Consisting of lots of suspense
But at times, they're a ferocious crocodile
And hit you like a missile
During every different dream, there's an unknown mystery.

Hannah Manish (10)
St Peter's CE Primary School, Harborne

Me And My Doggy

My doggy goes woof and I go hi
My doggy goes woof woof and I go bye
He pees on trees and rolls in leaves
He sleeps on a mat
He likes it flat
I sleep in my bed with my fluffy ted
I walk my doggy
When we get back, he is always soggy
I love my doggy, Roy
He is a very good boy.

Sofia Manea Vieira (7)
St Peter's CE Primary School, Harborne

Ted

Ted is a bear, white and bright
He walks around in brown and black clothes
He goes out in a hat and comes back with a sack
He goes for walks on sunny days
He eats honey and plays with money
Ted is a bear, white and bright,
He is not real but I love him tight.

Aleah Brkic (7)
St Peter's CE Primary School, Harborne

My Cupcake And Me

I walked in the kitchen and this is what I saw
A cupcake on the counter is what I adore
I kept my cupcake with me and took it to the sea,
It got stung by a bee and this is what we see,
A cupcake running home because it needed a cherry
And I finally ate it.

Gabrielle Challoner (7)
St Peter's CE Primary School, Harborne

My Cat

I have a beautiful cat,
On my leg it sat,
But it's so fat!
And it wears a purple hat
It knows how to catch a rat!

It loves to play and run
And we have a lot of fun
It likes to sleep under the sun
It's my number one.

Mariam Zaakouk (8)
St Peter's CE Primary School, Harborne

Don't Come To Me!

I'm a bee in the sea
And I'm drinking my tea
So don't look at me
Or I'll make you eat a pea
And well, you'll definitely see.

Deepika Kumari Sharma (7)
St Peter's CE Primary School, Harborne

Harry And Hogwarts

H ogwarts is the best school in the world
A nd Gryffindor is his favourite team
R on and Hermione are his best buddies
R unning from Voldemort
Y ou know Voldemort is the worst wizard in the world, the worst you can get.

H e got a letter from the school of witchcraft
O h, and wizardry
G ood luck to the first graders
W izards from this school and witches
A re all good ones except for one
R ight you are, Voldemort went to this school
T he leader of Hogwarts is Professor Dumbledore
S lytherin is the worst team in the world.

Lacie Humpage (8)
Widey Court Primary School, Crownhill

The Fat, Black Cat

Look at the feline, all round and chubby
When she spies, she hides her tummy
Look at the lioness, as she eats
Gobbling a packet of scrumptious treats
Look at the jaguar, as careful as a spy
Jumps off a sofa to fly
Look at the cat, so dark-souled
With all her blubber, she'll never get cold
See the tiny tiger, really slinky
When she pounces, it's so freaky
See the ponderer, pondering along
She hears gong, pause, shriek, scream then carries on
See the feline, so plump and fat
That's the story of the fat, black cat.

Owen Wren (8)
Widey Court Primary School, Crownhill

Space Adventures

I want to walk on the moon
And maybe visit Neptune
I wish on the stars
Or see the red of Mars
I travel in my spaceship very fast
And I land on the moon at last
I love to explore
It's fun not sitting on the floor
I like floating in space
It's a shame I haven't seen an alien's face
Oh no, the spaceship's fuel is getting low
I think it might be time to go
It's time to travel back to Earth
We're landing on AstroTurf.

Oliver Tozer (8)
Widey Court Primary School, Crownhill

Veruca Salt

Veruca Salt, a bit of a brat,
Who is as lazy as a cat,
She thinks she is a queen,
But actually, she is a horrid bean,
Her clothes are shiny like a new pin,
But after a day, it reaches the bin,
Talking about the bin, she went down the chute,
Like a cat doing a toot,
Her bedroom is very princessy
But actually, it is quite messy.

Georgia Horne (8)
Widey Court Primary School, Crownhill

Aliens

A wesome
L earning about Earth
I ncredible
E xciting
N aked
S inging happily.

Bethany Goodman (9)
Widey Court Primary School, Crownhill

YOUNG WRITERS INFORMATION

We hope you have enjoyed reading this book – and that you will continue to in the coming years.

If you're a young writer who enjoys reading and creative writing, or the parent of an enthusiastic poet or story writer, do visit our website **www.youngwriters.co.uk**. Here you will find free competitions, workshops and games, as well as recommended reads, a poetry glossary and our blog. There's lots to keep budding writers motivated to write!

If you would like to order further copies of this book, or any of our other titles, then please give us a call or order via your online account.

Young Writers
Remus House
Coltsfoot Drive
Peterborough
PE2 9BF
(01733) 890066
info@youngwriters.co.uk

Join in the conversation!
Tips, news, giveaways and much more!

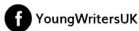 YoungWritersUK    @YoungWritersCW